WILDFIRE!

Ashley Wolff

BEACH LANE BOOKS
New York London Toronto Sydney New Delhi

Buck hears the rumble.

Squirrel sees the flash.

Jay spreads the news,

"FireFireFire in the forest!"

Turkey vulture spots the first wisp.
High in Spruce Mountain Tower,
Maria spots it too.

Radios crackle.

"Evergreen Dispatch to Red Bridge Crew:
Spruce Mountain Tower reporting light-colored smoke!"

"Roger that, Spruce Mountain. Calling out Red Bridge Crew!"

High on Spruce Mountain,
flames flicker through pine needles.
Doe nudges her sleepy twins.

Raven croaks,

"FireFireFire in the forest!"

Pilots get their launch orders.
Aircraft take off,
bellies full of water and retardant.

They follow the air attack plane,
all heading toward Spruce Mountain.

Coyote gives three sharp barks
and gathers his band.
They crawl into their den.

Redtail screams,

"FireFireFire in the forest!"

Mia banks her plane hard.
Parachutes bloom and float.
Smoke jumpers land and roll,
scrambling to their feet.
They rush to fight the fire.

Black bear feels the hot wind.

Calling her cubs, she wades into the bog.

Great gray owl hoots,
"FireFireFire in the forest!"

Red Bridge Crew roars into a burning meadow.

Don aims his nozzle, knocking down flames.

Brennan and his hotshot crew hack out a rough firebreak.

Porcupine hurries to hide.

Cougar hisses at a flaming branch.

Woodpecker chatters,

"FireFireFire in the forest!"

Air tanker circles, retardant billowing from cargo doors.
Helicopter follows, dumping a first load of water.

But flames still spread, driven by hot wind.
Tired crews are falling behind.

Turtles burrow in the mud.
Frogs hunker between rocks.

Wood duck quacks,

"FireFireFire in the forest!"

The forest crackles and booms.
Towering pines explode.
"Heads up, crew!" yells Brennan,
as one crashes across the fire line.

Rowan's bulldozer roars.
He plows a wide alley,
pushing fuel away from the flames.
The scraped earth finally halts the fire's march.

When darkness comes, the forest
is still bright with flames.
But the wind has dropped.
The fire line is holding.

A storm climbs Spruce Mountain,
dousing the flames.
Hot spots hiss.

Tired firefighters gather their gear and roll back to base.

Pilots fly through the night,
ferrying smoke jumpers to a new fire,
far to the south.

As the scorched ground cools,
doe searches for grassy meadows.
Squirrel finds an open cone stuffed with nuts.

Coyote and his band howl at the stars.

And life continues on Spruce Mountain.

AUTHOR'S NOTE

"Only *you* can prevent forest fires!" says Smokey Bear. The US Forest Service created Smokey in 1944 to get the American public to help with fire suppression efforts in the national forests. New firefighting technologies were developed, including airplanes, smoke jumpers, and the use of fire suppression chemicals. With these tools, fires could be fought anywhere—and they were. In the 1960s, new scientific theories about the role of fire in keeping a forest healthy resulted in big changes. Starting around 1970, a new "let burn" policy began to evolve, but the size and ferocity of fires since then has only grown. The Forest Service now spends up to 50 percent of its budget fighting fires, reducing funds for forest thinning and land restoration.

Fire is a natural part of the forest's regeneration system. Forests need fire to enrich the soil, spread seeds, let in more sunlight, and act as a natural disinfectant. Most forest trees need to be exposed to fire every fifty to one hundred years to encourage new growth. Forest management can include controlled burns. These slow-burning fires make room for new life that will help keep the forest healthy in the long term. Though it is widely known that fire can be good for a forest, most fires are still vigorously fought.

The fire in this book was started by a lightning bolt. But 85 percent of the wildland fires in the United States are caused by humans leaving campfires unattended, burning debris, using equipment like lawnmowers that create sparks, negligently discarding cigarettes, and intentionally setting fires. Fires are fought when they may threaten vulnerable ecosystems or populated areas.

Not all wildlife survive a forest fire, but healthy populations will recover. Dozens of species can live in recently burned forests and some species of birds and certain wildflowers and shrubs prefer this habitat. Some beetles even have heat-sensing organs to detect forest fires from miles away, rushing toward them to lay their eggs in the just-burned trees.

In recent years, forest fires have become much larger and more destructive due to a combination of climate change and human activity. The extremes of weather caused by climate change create hotter, dryer forests: perfect conditions for wildfires. At the same time, building in the fire-prone wildland–urban interface—the space between urban and wilderness areas—has become the fastest form of land use in the contiguous United States.

We can *all* help prevent forest fires by doing what we can to slow climate change and being very careful with fire.

FIREFIGHTING TERMS

Aerial firefighting: Using aircraft to combat wildfires. Aircraft can carry water, foams, gels, and fire retardants to fight the fire. If significant exposed water sources are nearby, planes and helicopters can scoop up buckets of water and carry them to be dropped atop the blaze. Water is often mixed with foam before being dropped. The solution acts as a more effective barrier to the spread of fire and also insulates fuel that has not yet burned.

Air tanker (or just **tanker**): Aircraft modified to drop fire retardant on or near a fire. Helicopters may be fitted with tanks (**helitanker**) or they may carry buckets of water.

Dispatchers: People who provide the communication link between the wildfire coordination centers and the aircraft, firefighters, and other people in the field.

Fire lookout: A person who watches for the first wisps of smoke so wildland firefighting resources can be dispatched as rapidly as possible. Using a single Osborne Fire Finder in conjunction with a digital elevation model, lookouts can radio coordinates to wildfire coordination centers and, moments later, firefighters, helicopters, and aircraft are on their way.

Fire retardant: Chemicals that draw a line in the landscape that can stop a fire from spreading while ground crews work to get it under control. The potent mix of chemicals in the most common type of retardant can leave scars of its own, polluting watersheds and harming the fish and other animals that live in them.

Firebreak: An area cleared of all flammable material to prevent a fire from spreading across it. Firebreaks may also be created by backfiring: creating small, low-intensity fires using drip torches or flares.

Fire line: The line where firefighters intend to stop a spreading fire.

Hand crew (or **crew**): A crew of firefighters who bring tools to the fire to make the job easier and to isolate the fire within a given area.

Hotshot crew: A crew of firefighters who use tools like chainsaws, axes, Pulaskis, and shovels to create firebreaks and isolate the fire within a given area.

Smoke jumpers: Wildland firefighters who parachute to the site of a forest fire. They are able to reach remote areas quickly and combat wildfires before they get out of control. Smoke jumpers must be in top physical condition and attend regular training courses.

Tactical aircraft: These command-and-control aircraft include fixed-wing planes and helicopters. The crews provide information on the movement and spread of the fire to the incident commander on the ground and can direct the air tanker and helicopter pilots where to make their retar-dant and water drops. The helicopter's infrared thermal imager can detect the heat from a fire even through thick smoke and provide precise GPS coordinates to ground crews and pilots.

Wildfire: An uncontrolled fire in a rural area with combustible vegetation.

FIREFIGHTING TOOLS

Boots required by the National Wildfire Coordinating Group must be eight-inch high, leather, lace type with nonslip, melt-resistant soles and heels.

Canteens are carried by firefighters since they may need one quart of water each hour while on the fire line.

Chain saws are are one of the most important firefighting tools. The firefighters who use them are called sawyers, and they are often in front, clearing a safe path for the rest of the crew. A sawyer depends on their saw, and one way of taking ownership is to give it a name. This Stihl MS461 is called Hot Dog.

Drip torches are used to set backfires, burnouts, and prescribed burns.

Fire shelters are a safety device of last resort used by firefighters when trapped by wildfires. While fire shelters cannot withstand sustained contact with flames, they can protect a firefighter's life in a short-lived blaze.

Headlamps help firefighters see at night.

Nomex shirts and pants are made of an extremely fire-resistant synthetic material created by DuPont in the 1960s.

The **Pulaski** is a special hand tool that combines an axe and an adze in one head.

Safety glasses or **goggles** protect firefighters' eyes from heat, sunshine, smoke, embers, dirt, and sawdust from cutting operations.

Wildland fire helmets protect firefighters' heads from sparks and falling debris.

Firefighters carry **wildland fire packs**, which include the fire shelter, food, water, a first aid kit, and all other items needed on the fire line.

SOURCES

Cal Fire
https://www.fire.ca.gov/programs/fire-protection/air-program/

Outside **magazine**
https://www.outsideonline.com/2397137/wildfire-smoke-health-risks
https://www.outsideonline.com/2289216/20-years-wildfires-will-be-six
-times-larger

Pacific Biodiversity Institute
http://www.pacificbio.org/initiatives/fire/fire_ecology.html

Science **magazine**
https://www.sciencemag.org/news/2020/09/wildfires-continue-western
-united-states-biologists-fear-vulnerable-species

US Forest Service
https://www.fs.usda.gov/science-technology/climate-change

US Forest Service resources for educators
https://smokeybear.com/en/for-educators/elementary-resources

For Brennan and all the strong and brave men and women
who protect our forests and wildlands

Special thanks to Glenn Flamik, retired California Department of Forestry and Fire Protection (CAL FIRE) forester, and Nick Canceco Renner, hand crew firefighter with the Banks Fire District in Oregon, for reviewing this book and sharing their expertise.

BEACH LANE BOOKS • An imprint of Simon & Schuster Children's Publishing Division • 1230 Avenue of the Americas, New York, New York 10020 • © 2021 by Ashley Wolff • Book design by Karyn Lee © 2021 by Simon & Schuster, Inc. • All rights reserved, including the right of reproduction in whole or in part in any form. • BEACH LANE BOOKS and colophon are trademarks of Simon & Schuster, Inc. • For information about special discounts for bulk purchases, please contact Simon & Schuster Special Sales at 1–866–506–1949 or business@simonandschuster.com. • The Simon & Schuster Speakers Bureau can bring authors to your live event. For more information or to book an event, contact the Simon & Schuster Speakers Bureau at 1–866–248–3049 or visit our website at www.simonspeakers.com. • The text for this book was set in Bailey Sans ITC. • The illustrations for this book were rendered in acrylic gouache on Arches cover paper. • Manufactured in China • 0721 SCP • First Edition • 10 9 8 7 6 5 4 3 2 1 • Library of Congress Cataloging-in-Publication Data • Names: Wolff, Ashley, author. • Title: Wildfire! / Ashley Wolff. • Description: First edition. | New York : Beach Lane Books, [2021] | Audience: Ages 0–8. | Audience: Grades 2–3. | Summary: Illustrations and easy-to-read text reveal the struggles of forest animals to survive when fire breaks out on Spruce Mountain, and the actions of the firefighters who work through the night to stop the blaze. • Identifiers: LCCN 2020055022 (print) | LCCN 2020055023 (ebook) | ISBN 9781534487734 (hardcover) | ISBN 9781534487741 (ebook) • Subjects: CYAC: Wildfires—Fiction. | Forest animals—Fiction. | Fire fighters—Fiction. • Classification: LCC PZ7.W821234 Wil 2021 (print) | LCC PZ7.W821234 (ebook) | DDC [E]—dc23 • LC record available at https://lccn.loc.gov/2020055022 • LC ebook record available at https://lccn.loc.gov/2020055023